BRIAN DOUGLAS BEVERLY

I'LL BE THERE AT THE TOP OF THE MOUNTAIN

Order this book online at www.trafford.com
or email orders@trafford.com

Most Trafford titles are also available at major online book retailers.

Print information available on the last page.

ISBN: 978-1-4251-5539-1 (sc)
ISBN: 978-1-4907-6672-0 (e)

Trafford rev. 12/01/2015

www.trafford.com

North America & international
toll-free: 1 888 232 4444 (USA & Canada)
fax: 812 355 4082

Also by Brian Douglas Beverly

HOBO

HOBO II
The Journey

ACKNOWLEDGMENTS

The research I've done for this short fiction novel was helpful. And it took considerable amount of time to explore it.

AUTHOR'S NOTE

Again I'd like to present to the reader, an entertaining story for his or her enjoyment.

I'LL BE THERE AT THE TOP OF THE MOUNTAIN

PROLOGUE

The mountain climbers are mid-way to the top. The first day they came from the ground up the stock after they made base camp near landing, there at the base of the mountain. And on the fist day, the mountain climbers are very much ready because in its reality the physical has overtaken the mental disorder one gets from being high up. This: the second day, after having slept the night through in a hammock secure on a ledge. They're able to press on more forward, climbing higher up, and getting beyond the halfway mark as the day passes. The face of the mountain at this point is like a rock covered with gravel. Dust whisks into their faces as dirt flies and the gravel spills down on them with each step they take. Now the experience each one of the five mountain climbers has gives them the confidence to keep going. They plan to reach the top of the mountain on the fourth day. So they're keeping watch on the time. They want to make each hour of daylight count, because it's too dangerous in the dark to see handholds and see where to place the pitons for attaching the ropes and pull them selves up. As well, they must rest again. Night has come, and this time they're sleeping in hammocks, hanging over the front of the cliff by way of the ropes.

The mountain climbers have nerves of steel. They can see as far as the eye can see while they lie there. The sun rises on the other side of the mountain and then comes over the top. It's the third day they're climbing up the face of the mountain, that's called the nose, on this mountain. And now it's raining. Still there can be no slipping down. One must keep steady on his way.

A Coshocton Dulge ranks highest on the mountain. He is able to climb the fastest and maintain good safety. There have not been any treacherous moments climbing the mountain so far. Night has fallen on the third day now. And again they will sleep in their hammock hanging from off the cliff. The wet from the rain and the high up weather, present some of the difficulty to their climb. But they've managed to get the low-angled places at this point on the cliff, so the body weight is to their feet, rather than so much of their arm strength. At the top of the mountain is the finish line. The hammocks are swaying as they hang in the night. The mountain climbers can hardly sleep this time. Still, they all will have rested enough for the last of the climb.

It's morning now, and they have just finished eating. Higher up the nose of the mountain they go. The cold and wet diminish in the afternoon. But it is still difficult to climb in the hottest part of the day. Coshocton Dulge reaches the top of the mountain first. The others all manage to make it to the top, as well. Now they will walk the trail that is on the other side of the mountain back to the base camp below.

1

High up in the skyscraper, here in Manhattan, New York, are slogan professionals. They are trying to come up with an advertisement for the computer industry executive in Massachusetts. They would like to have it intermix with another event.

"The bowling alleys are nice," the one at the podium suggests.

"Your display looks a bit like it—what we're after," says one of the others who's seated at the long table.

"I don't know. The bowling ball rolling down the lane and stopping in mid-air, to display the keyboard at your fingertips, that the ball is at your fingertips coming off, is a bit out of it for me," another speaks up.

"How's about me now—coming with what I

got?"

"Yes, Anthony Guster. Let's have yours. And you can step down now, Steven. We see what cha got, and we have you in mind," says Mister Cutrite who has the big business in New York and is seated at the head of the table. He is a rather large man sitting big and fat in his chair, with an unlit cigar in his mouth. The hair around his bald-head is black from dye and the plastic frames of his glasses are black, too. Because of his big size, his suit doesn't fit right.

"I'd like to impress upon you—roller skating in a roller rink," Anthony says as he brings the posters from out of his briefcase.

"As you can see, here, I have roller skating with the mouse out in front, like trying to catch a mouse, quick as he is, that a person is on skates," he continues.

"And it's in a roller rink, where skatin' mostly is. You sseee...the mouse, that you use at your computer is quick response," finishes Anthony Guster.

"Gentlemen, you're not too shabby of a bunch, except we're lookin' for something more in the outdoors. An event that goes on that way," says Mister Cutrite.

"Then perhaps you'll like my idea," says Walter Husband.

"Yes Walter, what is it?" asks Mister Cutrite.

"Welll...if I can step up to the podium, I'd be glad to share it with you."

"Of course, Anthony you step down now and we'll take a look at what Walter's got."

"Ok, Mister Cutrite."

After Anthony Guster takes his seat, Walter Husband gets the floor. He is a tall graceful man, age forty-five, and shaves all of the hair off the top of his head. In addition, Walter has a very thick mustache, and stands six feet, five inches tall. Walter can see very easily past all of the men seated at the long table and over the top of Mister Cutrite where there's a giant window behind him. Moreover, seeing out of the window, Walter Husband at the podium is looking at the top of tall buildings. And there's a bunch of them, like trees in a forest. The sky is grey from below, but up above the sun is out.

"Gentlemen, I'd like to impress upon you mountain climbing. I believe you'll find this to be the greatest outdoors event."

"Yes... Yes...just you go ahead Mister Husband," replies Mister Cutrite. The very distinguished Walter Husband is putting his pictures on the easel and is presenting his slogan. He is very experienced and confident in giving his presentation.

"I've got five pictures to show and tell; the first one is at the foot of the mountain, and will climb up to the top, showing it's advanced."

They have got all of their attention on the easel. As Walter tells each phase of the mountain climbers and showing the computer works in motion, they get the feeling of listening to an interesting fairy tale that behooves them.

A large group of people in Moab Utah is at their social gathering in the desert. The most prized ones are the kids. It has always been their time to get in touch and bring the parents together. Big thick juicy hamburgers and real beef hot dogs are sizzling on the grill, in the open outdoors.

And the air is filled with their outburst of excitement.

A father says to his nine-year-old son who's getting into shenanigans: "Little Milton you'd better stop what you're doing and behave!"

"Ok, dad!"

"That's good going—getting to the top of that rock Brent Bryson. You didn't let us down out here," replies the high school football coach who is in charge of some of the events. And the seventeen-year-old Brent Bryson is the quarter back for the team.

"I get to go next!" shouts a young girl aged eleven.

"No... it's my turn," says Dewey Johnson who is age ten.

"No sir! You got ahead of me, Dewey Johnson. You're supposed to be back there," she continues.

"That's right, Dewey!"

"Yeah Dewey, you did. So you just get back here with us."

The others chime in as though they were standing in line.

"Ok! Ok! Let her go ahead and you step back," the coach again. After Brent Bryson gets down off the rock, they fix her up in the harness and put her to it.

"I need to get a boost-up, to start!" she cries.

"There's Coshocton Dulge standing near ya. That's what he's for," replies the coach.

Coshocton can be found in a local gymnasium in town, and around the Nautilus system working out at the YMCA. He stands better than six feet tall, and is a well built-man, who looks confident in his man's way—to climb a mountain and reach out to the little ones—to believe in one's own self. Careful is Coshocton Dulge though, that his being attractive is luring. And he doesn't want to attract the ones who'll have him take up another kind of responsibility. He gives her a boost, and she takes to rock climbing right away. The crowd below is excited to see the young girl take to the event. However, halfway up the rock, it is as though she's grown too tired to keep climbing and slips down. She's hanging from the harness in mid-air. The Crane lowers her to the ground where Coshocton is standing so he can free her from the harness.

They all take turns at rock climbing. But there's a very different one coming. He's around the crowd and to the front, limping as he walks. The eight-year-old Arnold Caldwell has a clubfoot. It is Talipes Varus. His left foot is turned inward and rests on its outer edge. He weighs heavier than most eight-year-old kids; he stands four feet nine inches tall. Arnold is wise for his age and has good wits. He is also very shy, but his parents are of good cheer and keep him uplifted. Now, standing there looking up at Coshocton Dulge, he wants to climb the rock.

"I want to try," says Arnold.

"Maybe you can get up there," says Coshocton. "Come here and we'll see," he finishes.

Arnold Caldwell, with his clubfoot, walks limply over to him and gets fixed up into the harness. As he starts to climb, Coshocton tries to help him start.

"That's ok you don't have to help me."

"Alright then, you go ahead."

First stepping up with his good foot, Arnold starts to climb. He mostly pulls himself up with his arms then pushes trying with his good foot, to make-up for where he is lagging on the left side. He is reaching the halfway mark and the crowd below is cheering.

"That's it Arnold, you can do it!"

"Go ahead and climb-up!"

"You're halfway there now! Keep going!"

Arnold is at a stand still at the halfway mark and the crowd cools down. Coshocton Dulge isn't cheering, nor encouraging him to come down. He too is standing still—watching. Arnold Caldwell is hanging on tenaciously. He heaves up for the final time. He lets go and drops off, because he has to use his arms in place of his clubfoot-leg. Once lowered to the ground, Coshocton releases the harness, and the crowd applauds. Arnold's parents come over to where he is and take him to sit at a table and get a hamburger off the grill. A lot of them follow him and began with lunch. The picnic table is set with potato salad, pork and beans, coleslaw and their is sweet-corn on the cob. As well as what's cooking on the grill. Giant size bags of Potato chips and pretzels are available for snacking. Someone manages to bring ice-tea and lemonade, to drink, along with the big cooler full of soft drinks. A lot of the adults are already seated around the table.

"Your son was very impressive trying to climb up there," says a lady who is sitting across from Arnold and his parents.

"Yes we know," his mother says.

"Is his foot going to stay that way or can they fix it?" she asks.

"The doctors can fix it, but we're still having to save money to do so, in addition to what we get from insurance," his mother answers.

"Yes that's right. His clubfoot is anatomic abnormality. At first, they were treating it at the hospital with casting and physical therapy. But he really needs surgery," Arnold's father chimes in.

A little boy comes to the grill and asks: "Can I have a hotdog Mister Kinkaid?"

"Yes, but that's why I have 'em stacked in that big pan over there."

"Those are better ones up there, because they're hot."

"Yeah, sure kid, I tell ya what, get your hotdog bun and I'll fix you right up." Jimmy Kinkaid brings the sizzling hotdog from off the hot charcoals and places it on the boy's bun. And within minutes a little girl is there.

"Hey get me something too. But I don't want a hotdog, I want a hamburger."

"Oh...no...not another one," Jimmy Kinkaid replies.

"Yeah...umm...huh...I want it from there—hot, too."

"You know you're special, and since you are, you go get you a special hamburger bun, and then I'll put you one," he finishes.

Jimmy Kinkaid is a tall lanky man, who is sixty seven years old, and has a corner store in town called Jimmy's Market. He has gotten to know a lot of the town's people because of it. He dyes his hair black, yet some grey streaks still show. And his eye glasses on is face are thick and wide Black plastic rims with a thick glass in their center, thick as the bottom of a glass coca-cola bottle.

"Hey Miss Hopensack, he said I was special and get a special bun for my hamburger,"

"I heard what he said," she replies to the little girl as she is sitting there big and wide down on her seat.

Miss Hopensack, taking the bun from the plastic wrap, gives it to her saying, "Here this bun is special enough."

"Thank you. Now there Mister Kindcaid, here is my special bun."

"Oh...Well...good. And here's the hamburger."

"That's great!"

From a not too far distance away, comes Coshocton and the rest of the people to attend.

"Mister Kincaid! We're coming to get it off the grill!" shouts Brent Bryson approaching.

"I'm coming too!" shouts another.

"No you're not gonna attack this grill. I want all of you to get it from out of the pan that's over there on the table," Jimmy Kincaid commands back to them with his long finger pointing and the other hand up high over his hand with the spatula gripped tight and his baggy pants flapping in the

wind along with the white apron he's wearing. They all do as he says, but Coshocton Dulge and the coach are beckoned by some of the other men who is sitting at a table. To come over and sit with them and then they'll go for the food.

2

The morning has come and Walter Husband has just entered into the big business building in downtown Manhattan. He makes his way into the elevator and is going up to the top floor, to meet with the other executives. Towering up, the elevator makes frequent stops along the way, for the other passengers to disembark.

"That was a very interesting conversation we were having over by the water cooler, Anthony."

"I'd like to fill you in on some more of what they're doing in the libraries with computers now. But there's not gonna be enough time today."

"As soon as Mister Husband gets here we'll

start," says Mister Cutrite.

Just then, Walter Husband comes through the door of the conference room.

"Good morning Gentlemen," he replies.

"Good morning," says Mister Cutrite.

All of the rest of them gestured without speaking. Walter Husband then takes his seat and the business of advertising begins. It has to be decided which one of them gets the deal.

"Gentlemen as you can see Mister Donaldson, of Donaldson Techniques has been sitting in on this meeting with us. He's the investor. We'll hear from him first, before we give you our decision," says Mister Cutrite.

"Yes, its been very good—my coming here gents. I'd like to express to you that all of you did a fine job of presenting your slogans for our computer works. And I'm glad I came. Thank you Mister Cutrite," finishes Mister Donaldson.

"Very well then, if there's no more you'd like to say I'll get on with who we're gonna have the account. Walter Husband, that's you," says Mister Curite.

The executives seated around the table applaud as Walter takes the podium.

"Gentlemen, you've all heard my slogan at our presentation nearly a month ago. The mountain I choose to have for it is El Capitan, in Yosemite Park. But the mountain climbers are not yet known. Again, I wish to present to you, briefly just what it's going to be. At the start of the climb I'll have the mountain climbers going up, and the computer Tower will be intermixed in the picture taking as they climb. So will the keyboard with the mouse displayed just ahead of it on the next day at better than a quarter of the way up, then on the third day I'll have the flat screen climbing up with the mountain climbers. Finally, on the forth day at the summit, it'll be the Advance laptop computer mix with the pictures and filming of the mountain climbers on a real mountain. And it'll be the prettiest pictures with the best real scenery that you'll ever know for Advertisement," the final words coming from Walter Husband.

3

In Moab Utah a very pleasant and most exquisite day has dawned. And it is said the desert will grow on you. The pass time here one has in the day is unlike that in New York. Coshocton Dulge finishes eating his breakfast and walks outside of his house that is on the suburb of town. His street is full of houses. Still, he can see the desert past them. A Mercedes Benz comes to Coshocton and parks in his driveway behind his Rubicon Jeep Wrangler. A very beautiful brown-skinned woman gets out of the car and walks over to where he is standing.

"Good morning, Irene."

"Good morning to you." She embraces Coshocton and gives him a kiss. Then she follows him into the house and sits on the sofa. Irene Baker stands five feet seven inches tall, and is size seven. Her hair is black-down past her shoulders. She is a social worker and holds down an office in the town public building. Irene Baker is Coshocton's longtime girlfriend who wants to marry him. But he says it still takes time for that. "Today is Friday. It's still a weekday. Shouldn't you be at your office?" asks Coshocton.

"We made it through the audit with flying colors last week, so I got today off. I really put myself to it, and they're keeping their promise to me," says Irene.

"We'll have to find something to do with your long weekend."

"I thought we'd get married on Sunday."

"So that's what goes on inside that pretty little head of yours?"

"Don't you ever want to get married?"

"You don't just get married on a Sunday. There's supposed to be a preparation."

"We've long since been prepared by now."

They sit together on the sofa the rest of the morning. Coshocton manages to bring

up other topics to discuss. And in the afternoon both of them stroll through the city park arm-in-arm, together in thought.

4

Barbra Caldwell opens the front door to her house and finds a well-dressed businessman standing there.

"Hello Mrs. Caldwell. I am Doug Feathers of the Feathers Insurance Agency. Do you mind if I step inside and talk with you and your husband?"

"I'd like to know why."

"It's about your son Arnold and his condition."

"All right, come on in. Arnold's in the next room and so is his father. You can sit in that chair by the window."

As he sits down, she goes from the living room into the family room.

"I heard the door bell ring. Who is it?" asks

Frank Caldwell just as Barbra appears.

"It's a Mister Doug Feathers, from the insurance agency. He says he wants to speak to us about Arnold. I left him in the living room."

Arnold follows his parents and he is standing on his one good foot, the other is the clubfoot. His father goes over to greet Doug Feathers. "Hello there, I'm Frank Caldwell," After shaking hands everybody sits down. All of the Caldwell's are seated on the sofa, across the room from Mister Feathers.

"As I was saying to Mrs. Caldwell, I am here on behalf of Arnold's condition. I couldn't help but to hear you talking about it at the rock climbing event we had this summer."

"You mean the talk of paying for the operation?" asks Barbra.

"Yes, that's it. I'm able to start up a donation from my company. That is if you'd like to hear it."

"That sounds good, if my son can get corrected," replies Frank.

"Sure Mister Caldwell, what we'll do is

make up some posters asking for a donation. And put them in the big windows in some of the local businesses here in town, along with some big empty coffee cans, and see if they fill up enough times to get the operation."

They agree with Doug Feathers and accept his offer. The posters in the windows have a picture of Arnold from head to shoulders and reads: help an 8-year-old boy who has ANATOMIC ABNORMALITY. TALIPES VARUS. Still it's going to be a slow process. The money will be some small change from out of people's pockets or pocketbooks.

5

The summertime of the year here in Manhattan is just as warm as any other climate. People without air conditioning units have their windows open with fans placed in some of them. Night has fallen, and the city is lit up with its nighttime lights.

Two weeks have passed since Walter Husband was selected to put up the computer advertisement. He is in his penthouse suite, waiting for guests to arrive. For preparation, he has h'ordeuvres and cocktails. His suite is decorated with awards and many pictures concerning his career. Again, Walter is seeing the forest of buildings from out of a window. He is standing in the living room, looking past his terrace—the outdoors. The doorbell sounds and awakens Walter Husband from his nighttime–day dreaming. He goes for the door and opens it to find his fiancée, Marsha Lungsfur there in the corridor.

"Are you surprised to see me or what?" she asks Walter.

"No, I was just doing me some thinking, that's all. Come in from out of the hallway."

She steps inside and goes to the bar for a drink.

"Would you like one?" she asks.

"I'll wait until after the guests get here."

"I hope you don't mind if I do?"

"As long as you don't drink too much before they get here."

"I won't."

"How do you like the h'ordeuvres?"

"I was about to ask—where did you get them?"

"They come from a Craft services that's here in Manhattan."

"That's impressive. Everyone is going to apprcciate you tonight."

After all of the guests arrive, Walter pores

himself a drink and took to the h'ordeuvres. "I can see you're comfortable," says Anthony Guster.

"Yes, I'm very comfortable here," Walter replies.

"Are you going to fill us in on the rest of how you intend to go about it?" asks Steven Johnson.

"That's partly why I have all of you here," says Walter.

Anthony has brought his wife, and so has Steven. Tina MacIntyre isn't married and came by herself. Tina is the receptionist at the front desk, who has gotten to know everyone who works in the firm. And she is very pretty. Marsha refreshes her glass at the bar, and then sits where Walter is.

"The question has been asked how do I intend to go about it."

All of them seated in the living room now are silent and have their attention on Walter Husband.

"I'm going to California one week from today, to Yosemite, and round-up the mountain climbers from there. Because that's where the mountain to be used is."

He finishes telling them where it's going to take place and explains he wants it to be a four-day expedition and he can take just the pictures he's looking for, in Yosemite Park. After Walter Husband finishes explaining the ordeal, they talk about it until well after midnight that night.

6

Coshocton Dulge is rock climbing, and is at a high point on the rock. Its summit though, still has to be reached. He looks as if he's a gymnast performing at a tournament. The temperature in the desert at this time of the morning has not yet risen. Coshocton has climbed some of the biggest mountains.

He is concentrating on not looking down too much. Coshocton is three quarters of the way up the small mountain. He has stopped to take-in a moment. The rope at his middle used for a life line is drawn tight. And the one in his hand is wrapped around at the wrist as though he is gripped to the rock wall of the mountain. Looking up to its summit, and seeing pass that, is endless.

The openness of the sky fills him for the moment with deep emotion. It feels like he is entering heaven. Coshocton Dulge will soon discover his feelings of well being are because of Irene. It's love, and he too gives Love—she asks for his hand in marriage.

He comes close, and studies the rock face, then he's making his way up to the top again. First he'll get his feet in an opening and push up with his legs, at the same time reaching into a handhold. If there are no handholds, Coshocton will hammer a piton into the wall of the rock. Then he'll clip his rope to it. Pitons are a kind of metal spike driven in for a climber to secure the rope to. He is using a double rope because of the harsh jagged rock where he is climbing. The rope can get cut off from the abrasion.

A few days have passed since he and Irene had their walk in the park. On the other side of town from where Coshocton lives, Arnold Caldwell is riding his bicycle up and down the sidewalk in front of his house. He is looking forward to the day when he can be as normal as all of the other kids. But he can't help feeling scared of the visits to the

doctor. So his parents keep him close and help him understand what it'll be like after the operation.

"Hey Arnold wait for me," a little girl who lives near him comes after Arnold, riding a bicycle. He has applied his brakes and is standing with his bicycle propped between his legs looking back at her.

"I want to ride bikes with you."

"Alright, Wendy."

The two youngsters go staggering together one in front of the other—staying on the paved sidewalk.

"Say, Mister McDonald! Don't forget to put your donation in the can before ya go," says Jimmy Kinkaid.

"Oh Yes, I see that. It's for the Caldwell boy with the clubfoot."

"Yes, that's right, helps out with what insurance won't cover."

"Sure... it's for a worthy cause. I can see everyone else that's donated could only put a few pennies like I am."

"Every little bit helps." Mister McDonald puts some coins into the coffee can, then leaves Jimmy Kinkaid's store. That night,

Irene drives to Coshocton's house after she's been to her condominium. The time in the day when she is at work, is their time apart. Sometimes Irene sleeps the night through at Coshocton's house. The both of them are lying together on the sofa, wrapped in each other's arms, kissing and caressing. And music is playing. They put a Jazz selection in the CD player.

"You don't have to propose to me again. Of course we'll be married," says Coshocton pulling himself apart from her just to say that.

A big beautiful smile fixes across her face—she is very pleased. The phone is ringing now, just as Irene is about to say something.

"Wait, let me go for the phone," he replies. Then he untangles himself from being wrapped around her.

"Yes, who is it?"

"Hello Coshocton, it's me, Joyce. I want to talk to Irene."

"Can you call back later?"

"Is that Joyce?" Irene asks.

"Coshocton, put her on the phone please!"

"Yes it is. Here, come and get it."

Irene gets the phone from Coshocton and goes over to the CD player and turns the music down.

"Hello Joyce, me and Coshocton was deep into our communications just when you called."

"I'm sorry to have barged in, so to speak. But I have you on my mind because of the party I'm having this Saturday. It's just us get 'n together so I need to touch base with you on that, and see what you have planned to help me out with it."

Joyce is Irene's lifelong girlfriend. They grew up together here in Utah and graduated at the same time from the same high school. Joyce is a registered Nurse at the town's main hospital and even though she's in the medical field, Joyce has a weight problem and she is conscientious about her size.

"I thought we'd order some pizza," says Irene.

"Oh no, not pizza. That'll make me gain weight," Joyce replies.

Coshocton goes into the kitchen so he can raid the refrigerator.

"Today is Monday, what did you two find

to do on a Monday?" asks Joyce.

"Really Joyce, you shouldn't have called. But you did, so ole' well."

The girls talk a bit more about the party. Another subject comes about and keeps Irene talking on the telephone, so the mood set for romance, diminishes. Coshocton is in the kitchen now and manages to fix himself up a sandwich using cold cuts.

7

Two representatives from Feathers Insurance agency are collecting the donation money from the business. They're spilling the cans into a large white cloth money bag. After having emptied all of them, the two girls make their way back to the agency.

"Susan and Charlotte are back with the donation money for the Caldwell boy."

Doug's wife Priscilla relays the message to him in his office from the conference room using the phone intercom. They've already spilled most of it from out of the bag onto the big long table. "That looks pretty good," says Doug Feathers as he enters.

"It's a lot of little stuff, but people are donating, so they care about it," replies

Susan.

"Well... let me know how much it is when you finish counting," Doug says.

The girls nod their heads and keep counting as he makes his exit.

"There's a lot of pennies here," says Charlotte.

"That's from the change back after they've paid for what they're purchasing," says Priscilla.

"Are we going to put all of this in coin rolls, or take it to one of the machines?" asks Susan.

"That's a good question," answers Charlotte.

"I think to roll it up because the machines take a percent. And besides that, the banks will most likely take our money rolls, on behalf of us being an Insurance agency to represent," Priscilla finishes.

"I'm ready to start rolling now. Because look at all of these stacks of coins and its just sixty two dollars, and forty eight cents," Susan replies.

"Here's some paper money. I have three five dollar bills, twenty-one singles, and someone put a ten," says Charlotte.

"I have some paper money here, too. And some of the donation is still in the bag," says Priscilla.

There are four other agents, not including Doug Feathers. And it is very busy this time of the day. Two of them sitting at their desk are working double time because Susan and Charlotte are involved else where. The telephones are ringing and customers are waiting longer than what's expected in the lobby.

"Just this much more to count. And then we'll have it," says Susan spilling what's left in the bag onto the table top. The ladies reach with their hands and rake the money to them as evenly as they can. Within just a few moments, they've counted, and have its total.

"This has come up way short," replies Priscilla." "Well...anyways, I'll go to Doug's office and tell 'em, rather then use the intercom," she finishes.

She leaves the conference room and goes down the hallway through the lobby to go through another hallway that leads to her husband's office.

"Hey Doug. We've got the money counted," Priscilla says after she reaches the open door. He has the phone to his ear and gestures her to wait until he hangs up the telephone. Priscilla stands back away from his desk, holding the paper held with the money count. Now he's put the receiver back in position.

"How much did we come up with?" he asks.

"It's that much in moneys," she answers handing him the paper.

"That's a ways from it."

"That's what I said back in the conference room."

"Yes, I see. Today's Thursday, so we still have this weekend to look forward to," says Doug.

"Should we wait until after that to notify the Caldwells?" asks Priscilla.

"Yes, let's wait until then," he answers.

The next day a plane lands in Fresno, California that has Walter Husband on board. He has disembarked the plane, and walks through the terminal, and goes to rent a car and drive to Yosemite Valley that has Mount El Capitan. Walter is taking in the good clear view of the wooded forest. There are the big evergreens and all types of flowers in their fullest bloom. The campers in the forest are a pleasant sight for Walter, too. He now is parking the rental car at the Yosemite View lodge where he'll be staying, and makes his way to the front desk.

"Hello sir, how may I help you?" asks a very pretty young woman, who is attending the reservation guest list.

"I'm Walter Husband, and I have a reservation."

She confirms his information and makes the transaction, and then Walter gets the key and goes to his room. He puts the suitcase on the bed, and lays his garment bag down on it as well. He unzips both of them and gets his clothes out of the suitcase, then puts them in the bureau and hangs his suits up in the closet. Now Walter comes into the shower. After that he plans to contact the park ranger that'll drive him around for his special event and look for a list of mountain climbers so he can select the ones for the slogan. The shower brings Walter back to life, after it's been the flight from New York to Fresno and then the two and a half hours' drive in the rental car. Once after he's toweled off, Walter gets the memo pad from his briefcase for the park ranger phone number—Walter makes the arrangement to meet there in the lobby. He comes into the lobby with long strides, and loads of confidence.

"You're the ranger, I take it?"

"Yes that's me," she answers standing there displayed in her uniform with her hand extended.

"I'm Walter Husband."

"Hi Walter, my name is Mitzy."

They shake hands and talk more about the arrangement.

"Did you want to review the list here, now? Or go for some sightseeing and look it over in the van?"

"Let's go to the van, and take me to the mountain, as well."

The first of the sites is the park, where there are campers moving about. And further into the drive, a deer appears on the side of the road.

"I gotta look out for that deer. Because they'll cross the road just as you're going past," says Mitzy.

Walter moves his eyes from the list of climbers and sees the deer standing there. It's a good clear day, that has the sun light glistening through the trees and the fully bloomed flowers color the forest with bright pretty pigments of yellow, whites, reds, and some pink ones distributed throughout the rest of the colors.

"The deer is staying there," says Walter.

"Good! That's good!" Mitzy sounds off.

The road leads more into the park and the up and down hills full of evergreen, has its canyon like ditches.

"I can see bears over there," says Walter.

"I see 'em, too. The park is full of bears. We have strict rules in the picnic areas and the campgrounds to secure your food so it doesn't attract the bears and to be sure not to leave the trash cans uncovered. The bears always know where there is food."

Walter brings his camera to take pictures of the mountain. He leans out the window as they're driving past the bears with the camera on the ready and takes a picture. In just a few more minuets, they reach El Capitan. Mitzy is putting the van in park. She and Walter Husband disembark and walk to the front. They stand looking at the face of the mountain.

"Well, there she is," says Mitzy,"

"That's high-up, isn't it?" asks Walter.

"Yes, its three thousand feet from where we're seeing it, and that's the nose."

"That'll be good enough for what I've got going on. Let me take just a few more pictures, and then we'll go back to the hotel. And I'll look over the list of mountain climbers better there."

Arnold Caldwell is at the boulder climbing in the desert along with others on this Saturday afternoon. He wishes to become an official boulder climber and a rock climber someday.

"Hello everyone, did you see in the paper about the donation that's for me?" Arnold asks.

"Yes I saw that," answers Coshocton Dulge.

"Well think of me if you will, because I need to have the operation."

"I will," says Brent Bryson.

"Yes I will Arnold, I will especially since you're trying to be a climber like I am," says Coshocton.

Irene and Joyce have decided to get party foods from the deli at the local grocer. It's the giant size vegetable tray, and a platter of cold cuts, with a mixture of different kinds of bread and snack crackers. Coshocton is holding down a conversation with some of the guests at the party. The main attraction is a big white sheet cake that Joyce plans to cut and serve to her party guests later in the evening.

"Do you like being an x-ray technician?" Coshocton asks Karl.

"It's a job. I was real interested in High Tech electronics when I first got into it. But now I just go to work."

"I see. I'm doing well in recreation. I was boulder climbing earlier today and we had a few people show up. There's this young boy with a clubfoot named Arnold Caldwell. A collection is being taken up for him so he can get his operation on his foot. I'm gonna try and help 'em. They want me to help with

the sports at the small college we have here and get paid for it. I've got my master's in Physical Education," says Coshocton.

The party guests are co-workers of Joyce's, and some neighbors she's gotten to know over the years living on her street. Everyone of the invited guest showed up that's suppose to. And that makes the party a success. The weekend comes to a close and again the donation money for Arnold Caldwell is collected and taken to Feathers Insurance agency.

"Well, there you two are," replies the receptionist in the lobby.

"Yes, we're in with the donation money," says Charlotte as she and Susan walk past.

"Get Priscilla for us. We'll be in the conference room," says Susan.

They put the money bag down on the table after they enter the conference room, and wait for Priscilla. Within just a few moments, Priscilla comes quickly where Susan and Charlotte are seated.

"Hello girls, would you say it's better this time?" asks Priscilla.

"Yes, there's more since it's been the

weekend," answers Susan.

"There's still a lot of nickels and dimes though," says Charlotte.

"Ok, we'll have it going on as best we can. If it's not going to be enough, then they'll still have to come up with their own solution," finishes Priscilla.

The money is counted, and Doug Feathers comes into the conference room himself to speak about the matter. He's decided to contact the Caldwells this time. Now, he comes from the conference room and goes to his office, with Priscilla trailing behind. He sits at his desk and picks up the telephone. Priscilla sits in a chair in front of the desk. Barbra Caldwell is in the upstairs putting the covers back on the beds and cleaning. And she will go to the kitchen to clean up the breakfast.

"When I was boulder climbing last Saturday, I asked everyone if they knew about the donation for me," says Arnold.

"What did they say?" asks Frank.

"They said they'd try for me. And Coshocton really seemed like he would."

Arnold and his father Frank Caldwell are

outside in the backyard enjoying the first of the daylight. The telephone is ringing, and Barbra answers it in the master bedroom upstairs.

"Hello, who is this please?"

"Mrs. Caldwell, this is Doug feathers. Did I catch you at a busy time?"

"Well... as a matter of a fact, you did. I'm cleaning up. But I know the reason you're calling. And I'm not too busy for you."

"Ok then, let's us just get down to it. The donation money has been collected and I'll tell you now, you're still a ways from it. But it does show a good difference."

"I do appreciate you people for your help. The matter concerning my son means everything to us, that he doesn't spend the rest of his life with a clubfoot."

"Yes, that's right. We'll keep going with the cans in the businesses, since it's only been just this past week. And they should gain some more."

"That sounds great! Frank and Arnold are together around here somewhere. I'll be sure and tell them you called."

"Ok, let's hang up."

She goes down the stairs right away and steps outside to find them with baseball gloves on their hands playing catch—throwing a hardball. Barbra tells them about the talk she just had with Doug Feathers. Afterwards she goes back inside to finish cleaning house and let them get back to what they were doing.

The middle of the week is busy. The gasoline stations are filled up with vehicles of every kind. And the grocery stores have long lines of people waiting to check-out. The traffic is jam packed in the streets. Mister Cutrite is sitting at a table near the front door of his favorite Manhattan New York restaurant for lunch. He has three of his business associates with him.

"I heard from Walter Husband last week on Friday," says Mister Cutrite.

"That's right, he's in Yosemite Park about his slogan," replies one of his associates.

"Yes, and he said he'll call again on Thursday, which is tomorrow," Mister Cutrite finishes. There is a plate of pasta down on the table for Mister Cutrite. And he has buttered French bread along with a

tossed salad. Fried bass is served to the associate on his right, along with mashed potato's and green beans. The one to his left thought of pasta too. So he asks for linguine. And the associate who's seated directly across from Mister Cutrite gives in to the very large bowl of home made Chicken noodle soup. A basket of dinner rolls is placed at the center of the table along with some butter.

8

It's the last business day of the week, and Coshocton is climbing a Utah mountain with a team of mountain climbers, in Zion National Park. They are very high up—close to the summit. And two of them on the team have developed AMS from climbing too high too fast. The body needs time to adjust to the oxygen when making a large increase in altitude. AMS is Acute Mountain Sickness, some call it altitude sickness.

"I still got ta wait a minute because my stomach is too queasy, like I'm gonna vomit. And this headache I got is bad,"

"Yeah ... that's it—AMS. You got it."

Coshocton in the lead has just placed a bolt piton, to take a safe step. He

clips his rope to it and is looking at his team of climbers.

"Who else has it?" he shouts.

"It's me over here too. I got dizziness, and shortness of breath."

"We're in good shape right here, to take time out," says Coshocton.

It isn't long after they rested that the climb is over. Almost all of them feel the effects of climbing too fast. They get shortness of breath from only walking about. Some mountain climbers take Diamox to prevent or relieve their AMS. Diamox is a sulfa drug. One can get a severe reaction from a sulfa drug. Coshocton Dulge has seen it happen before, and a particular man who climbs mountains with teams that Coshocton's been a part of got bad feverish from Diamox. He had to go see a doctor. So Cosocton doesn't use it. It's also talked among the other climbers that you can develop a rash or get bruises and a bad sore throat. So the ones climbing mountains who don't use Diamox are the very good ones.

On saturday Coshocton and Irene can hardly wait to see each other. He only talks to her on the telephone after the climb. Coshocton drives to her condo this afternoon-morning, and they position themselves on the love seat in Irene's living room.

"We've been out of touch this week, since you went away," says Irene.

"That's how's come I had to come right over," says Coshocton. Irene can't take her eyes off him.

"Good, because I know you missed me," she says staring into the side of his face as Coshocton keeps looking ahead. Now he turns to Irene and gives her a kiss.

"Let's go into the bedroom," she says.

After they kiss, she takes him by the hand to lead the way.

And on this Saturday, the open stores are filled up with people and there's a lot of change given back to people once after purchase—filling up the giant size coffee cans for Arnold's clubfoot operation.

Joyce has just topped off with fuel and can't help but notice the poster in the window, that's written in big bold letters. And that it's a picture of Arnold Caldwell with smaller writing asking for donations. She hangs up the nozzle and goes inside the gas station.

"I want to know more about the sign that's

posted in the window," she says approaching the cashier clerk behind the counter.

"That's for a youngster here in town, because the insurance is not enough. There's a coffee can here on the counter where people are making their donation, if you'd like to donate."

"Ok, I'll put something in."

Joyce puts in a five dollar bill and then makes her exit. She drives two miles from the gasoline station through town to wind up at Irene's place of residence.

"Don't you forget, tomorrow you're cooking me a good Sunday dinner at my house," says Coshocton as he's lying there in bed next to his fiancé.

"Oh yeah, that's right," she responds.

"Did you forget it?" he asks.

"Yes and no. Right now I'm thinking of us," Irene answers.

The doorbell sounds and Irene springs out of bed. She puts on her robe to answer the door. She comes out of the bedroom and goes to the living room window. Looking out the window, she can see Joyce standing there.

"Come in Joyce," Irene motions her in as she opens

the door.

"I came over to tell you about my gall bladder patient that I was having trouble with."

"Oh, is she getting better?"

"Yes, she finally got the will to live and I'm very pleased about it."

"That's good, I'm glad to hear it."

"She's an older woman is what it was."

Coshocton comes out of the bedroom with his pants on and his button-up front shirt is open.

"Joyce, you're staying. Leave," he says.

"Don't say that Coshocton," Irene pleads.

"She always calls or stops by at a bad time."

"That's ok Irene, I'll come back another time," Joyce says smiling at Coshocton.

"Wait, there's one more thing. I'm Arnold Caldwell's nurse when he comes to the hospital for therapy. I saw a poster in the window at a gas station asking for donations to help get his operation," Joyce finishes.

"That's in the news paper too. I hope someday I can help 'em. He wants to climb like me," says Coshocton.

Coshocton doesn't stay the whole night long with Irene. But it is after mid-night when he leaves her condo. The next day is risen and it's in the afternoon. Irene is at the grocery store getting what she needs to prepare the special meatloaf for Sunday dinner. The sun's love is coming through the bedroom window with the curtains drawn at Coshocton's house. He is lying on his side in bed, restless looking out of the window—a pleasant shining that's endless in the daytime.

It's gonna be good out today, he is thinking as he lies there."

Irene has just disembarked her Mercedes, and is walking to the front door. She uses the key Coshocton gave her to unlock the door and enters in. Once inside, Irene shouts for him as she goes to the kitchen.

"Hey, are you awake yet?!"

"Yes! I'm just lying here!"

"That's ok, lazy around on a Sunday." He stirs a bit and rolls over, then gets out of bed. He's yawning as he stretches, reaching up to the ceiling, then heads for the bathroom. Irene has placed all of the food

and spices on the countertop for cooking and has staged the pots and pans she intends to use. She is wearing a colorful flowery dress, with its hem just above her knees. Her shoes are brown pointy–toes and have two inch heels. Irene is very pretty with her hair perm and straight length down her back. Also, she manages to slip into an apron after she enters the kitchen.

Coshocton comes out of the shower and dries off using a towel, then puts his robe on and goes into the kitchen.

"You sure are beautiful today," he says holding Irene from behind her and brings his face around to kiss her cheek.

"Thank you. I'm feeling good, too. Why don't you go get dressed Coshocton? And stay out of the way so you don't see what I'm going to do to this meatloaf. It's my own special recipe."

"First turn around, then I will," she turns to him and gives him a hug and a kiss. The feelings of romance come over them, but Irene backs off and gets on with preparing the meal and Coshocton goes back to his bedroom to get dressed.

9

The day is moving along and Coshocton is in the family room watching a Major League Baseball game on television.

"It's ready! Come sit at the table!"

The table is covered with a white satin tablecloth and the dishes are white porcelain with bright shining sterling silverware. There are two white long stem-candles lit. He comes to the table and sits at the head of it. Irene has already placed the vegetables, which are the big bowl of broccoli and carrots. And mashed potatoes are next to a medium-sized bowl of gravy. There's also a large pitcher of fresh-squeezed lemonade.

"Where's the meat loaf?" asks Coshocton.

"It's still in the oven. I just haven't

brought it out, yet. First I put the vegetables—now I'll go get the meatloaf."

She goes back into the kitchen and leaves Coshocton sitting there. He is feeling very proud of her, because she fixed this meal all by herself for them. She lit the candles too, he is thinking.

Irene comes back into the dining room with the steaming hot meatloaf still in the oven pan. She places it down on a wooden cutter board that's centered on the table and takes her seat at the opposite end of Coshocton.

"Honey, this is great."

"You haven't tasted it yet."

"I can hardly wait."

"First let's say a prayer Coshocton and then we can eat."

He prays a positive and wishful prayer over the food. After that Irene reaches across and uncovers the main course. Then she rises from her chair and gets the carving knife and long handled fork and cuts half the meatloaf into slices. Once the plates are filled with food, she takes her seat and says

"Dig-in"

The first to get tasted is the meatloaf. Both of them have taken a bite and are using their fork to move the vegetables around on their plates. All of a sudden the telephone is ringing.

"I wonder who that is?" says Irene.

"Oh, you know who it is," says Coshocton.

"You mean to imply its Joyce."

"Yep, and like I said, she interrupts."

"You keep eating and I'll answer the telephone," Irene says laughing. "Besides, I'd like you to tell me about the meatloaf."

He takes another bite of the meatloaf as she goes into the living room.

"Coshocton, where's the telephone? I can hear it ringing but I don't see it!"

"It's in the bedroom on the nightstand. I had it in there last."

She runs into the bedroom and grabs the receiver from off the top of the phone.

"Hello, Coshocton Dulge's residence."

"Coshocton Dulge the mountain climber?"

"Yes that's right, he climbs mountains."

"Good, my name is Walter Husband. I am calling on behalf of a slogan I'm doing for computer industries executives in

Massachusetts. If Coshocton is available, I'd like to speak with him."

"Just one minute and I'll give him the phone." Irene comes hurriedly from the bedroom and swoops into the dinning room.

"Here, answer the telephone, and it's not Joyce, either." He puts his fork down on his plate and gets the telephone from Irene. Coshocton drinks some lemonade to clear his mouth and throat before he can answer the phone.

"Coshocton speaking."

"Good afternoon—evening your time. I am Walter Husband of New York slogans. At the present, I'm calling from Yosemite Valley in California. And what this is in regards to is an advertisement plan I have for computer industries executives in Massachusetts. Are you with me so far?"

"Yes, I'm with you."

"Good. Then we'll continue. I managed to get a list of mountain climbers here, with your name on it. I want the slogan to have real life pictures of mountain climbers climbing a mountain.

"You mean El Capitan, since you're in

Yosemite?"

"Yes that's right."

"I took a team up that mountain last year."

"I see the date here. And if you'd be interested in coming to an interview I am having here along with nine others, then I'll give you the rest of the details."

"Yes, I'm interested."

"Ok, and you know if you are selected to get your team back up again, then this will reward you quite nicely."

Coshocton is well with what Walter told him. He asks Irene for a pen and paper to write down the information. Walter explains he wants to start not long after the interview, that he wants them all to come prepared. Coshocton pushes the end button on the telephone after they finish talking and is telling Irene about their conversation.

"Walter Husband let me know in his own way some good pay is involved for whoever gets selected after the interview. And to come prepared to start then."

"That's great. How much money is it?"

"He didn't say exactly, but you know, if its

rewarding enough, I'm going to help Arnold Caldwell. I won't tell that to anyone else yet, first I got to get selected."

They finish eating and complete the evening with more romance after the special meatloaf dinner.

10

Whenever Coshocton goes to Yosemite Park, he's overtaken by the giant granite gorge—El Capitan, that can be seen from all points of the national park. It's a mountain three thousand feet high and one mile wide. Coshocton enters into the view lodge and finds Walter Husband. He is standing there in the lobby talking to seven of the mountain climbers who already showed up.

"I can see right off this is the man to know," says Coshocton after he goes up to Walter Husband with his garment bag and suitcase in hand.

"If you're a mountain climber it is," says Walter.

"I'm Coshocton Dulge."

"Good, I'm glad you made it." Coshocton puts his suitcase down on the floor and is shaking hands with Walter.

"Everyone, this is Coshocton Dulge, and I do remember it's Moab Utah, where I called."

"Yes, that's right," answers Coshocton.

They acknowledge his presents there and he lets go of Walter's hand, then gets his suitcase.

"Come over to the front desk, and I'll get you signed in to your room. You'll sign this roster now, and then there'll be one at the interview tomorrow morning." The other two mountain climbers arrive moments after Coshocton gets registered for his hotel room that night. They're all gathered together sociably at a table in the restaurant.

"I climbed the five thousand feet southeast face of mount Dickey, in Ruth Gorge Alaska, six months ago," says one of the mountain climbers.

"I went on an expedition in Alaska at mount saint Elias, about that long ago myself," replies another.

"A couple of weeks ago I was climbing in Zion National Park. Other than that, I was only doing some rock climbing in Utah. But I was here climbing El Capitan last year with a team," says Coshocton.

They've all shared their experiences with Walter Husband sitting there. And finished eating and got one last cup of coffee before going to their hotel rooms. A new day begins with birds of music and the sweet smell of blossoming flowers. And in the glistening sun light a very green caterpillar is crawling up a twig on a sycamore tree that's in Irene's backyard. She comes outside barefoot and dressed in her blue jeans with a big sweltering button-up front shirt. Irene walks off the patio and into the green grass.

"I love you Coshocton. And you'd better come back home to me and not get careless climbing that mountain, that you got picked out for," she says with the telephone gripped tight in her hands and pressed against her ear.

"Yes I know, and I need you too."

He is in his room sitting upright in bed.

"Do you want me to tell Arnold Caldwell that you'll help with the donation now?" she asks.

"Yes, you can tell 'em."

After he and Irene talk, Coshocton gets his team together and makes base camp. There are four other climbers to make a total of five. They put enough supplies to last four days at base camp, and make plans to climb up the mountain the easiest way, which is to take the same route as they did, before. Stretching up as high as he can reach, Coshocton is placing another piton to clip his rope onto. He is already hanging off a piton supported in a little sling ladder for the type of climbing they're doing—aid climbing. And on this first day of the climb, they manage to get all of their gear up to the top of the ropes. The hard work in the course of that wearies the climbers. The point to reach on the first day of the climb is a ledge, after they've completed three pitches. Donna, who is climbing up from underneath Coshocton and to his left is overjoyed about making it to the top, because it's going to be used for an advertisement. She is a stocky girl who's strong enough to keep up with some men in weight lifting at the gymnasium. Her hair is dark brown in color and she wears glasses.

"Say there Roy Roger, you better be sure and take the best pictures of me for the magazine," she shouts at one of the climbers to their right and has been given a camera to use along with the photographers below.

"And me, too." Ben, who is to Coshocton's extreme left just above Donna, sounds off.

"I will, don't you worry, it'll be the best picture taking ever," says Roy.

"You got issued a camera too, didn't you Ben?" Roy again.

"Yes, and I can assure you these shots I took so far are good ones. Even the pictures of you Milton, all the way over there," Ben finishes. Milton like Roy is climbing to the right of Coshocton beneath him. They've reached the ledge and will set-up the hammocks to bivouac there on the wall tonight. There are some mice moving about, they live in the cracks and ledges on El Capitan Mountain. And there is some plant life from where there is water coming through the surface of its vertical tower. Walter Husband below with his photographers is using a telescope to see them. Walter has a pair of binoculars hanging from around his neck, as well. The big boom cameras with their stacked-on lens are carefully placed on tripods and positioned to keep their aim at the mountain climbers. Night is falling here in Yosemite Valley, so they have all bed down for the evening. The next start of the climb has a lot of scallops, which are small holes that can be used to drive the piton into.

"These scallops ain't deep enough for my steel pitons so I'm gonna use my copperheads," says Coshocton.

"Ok, but you know to watch it with those copperheads, they're too soft to hold you if you fall—they'll break loose. They'll just only have your body weight," says Donna.

They all climb up to the next ledge putting rivets and bolts as Coshocton puts one copperhead after another. It takes the biggest part of the day and there's another ledge to reach before nightfall and that'll be the point before nightfall at this time, and they know its two pitches away.

"Before we get going again, I want to sit on this ledge and free my mind. That was a lot of concentration and my body is drained," says Roy.

Roy is a slender built man, age thirty five, who races cars—in Daytona Beach, Florida. After they've rested Coshocton climbs nineteen feet where he comes into some diorite flakes. He is driving pitons and using some bolts and rivets, then hooking across.

"I see Coshocton stopped there. What ya looking at Coshocton?" asks Milton.

"I'm looking at what's above us before we reach the next ledge. I remember the wall is blank there; it gets without flakes and cracks. We're gonna have to use the hand-drills and do a lot of hammering. And I can see a bunch of plant life coming up your way Ben," says Coshocton.

"Yeah, I can see it too," says Ben.

Ben is highly intelligent and has his Ph.D. in Mathematics.

"No it's not here in this particular spot. Last year when we climbed El Cap from here, you couldn't see the good places to put a spike until you got upon 'em," Roy replies.

"I remember it!" Milton shouts.

It's as though the mountain invited them

because of what Roy and Milton remembers. And the mountain climbing is flowing with each move and whatever safe or spike that gets placed. Donna is climbing up the rope Coshocton has carefully placed with a belay attached to his harness in case she falls, and he is feeding the rope trough the belay.

"Hay you big bird! You get out of here! Ben is punching at a Condor that's attacking him.

"Ben look out here it comes again!" Donna cries.

Whoosh...swoop...flying in flapping its wings and wild after him. The Condor is trying to bite Ben with its sharp bill.

"You're almost to the ledge Ben! Reach for that small tree that's above you!" Roy lets loose and screams at Ben.

"Ok Roy! I'll see if I can make it now since the Condor backed off me."

"You better hurry, it looks like he's circling in on you again," says Donna.

"Alright, I'm moving out. I'm at a good place here. I can see just up from this two-foot branch is the ledge."

"Wait Ben! Don't grab that branch! There's

a nest and it's got eggs in it!"

Coshocton standing upon the ledge can see why the Condor's attacking. Ben now has to change direction, so he decides to cross over to where Donna is.

"That's right, come my way!"

"Oh boy! Here he comes again! She I mean! After I fight it off this time, I'll cross over just that much away from the nest and then go up to the ledge from there."

The big bird comes in attacking, and Ben almost falls. Hanging on, he manages to reach with one hand and make a fist, and then strikes a blow that puts the Condor back in flight. Walter Husband and his crew below have crowded around the telescope.

"Let me see with your binoculars Walter!" One of the crewmembers asks excitedly because Walter has taken over the telescope.

"That should hold 'em for awhile, see what you can do?" says Coshocton from upon the ledge with his rope attached. The Condor is circling in open air as if to give Ben a chance to retreat. Milton on the other side gets to the ledge just moments after Coshocton does, and then comes Roy. Now

all of them rest there looking out at the open skies—watching the Condor come to her nest and sit on the eggs to hatch.

"Well...it's all the way to the top from here," Donna replies.

"That's right, it's all the way to the top now," says Roy.

"Let's bring up some food and water that's down on the other ledge," Milton suggests.

Milton and Roy pull the lifeline up to the ledge on the nose of El Capitan where they are now. Milton is a not so very tall man with powerful legs and arms who wears his hair long. He owns a small airplane that has one propeller. Resting there, they can see hundreds of feet of a hard grainy igneous rock that surrounds them. The sun becomes a big orange-red ball in the sky and brings the clouds down to where the mountain climbers are. Day two is at its end and they've finished eating. They get the hammocks out of their backpacks so they can bivouac at this point.

11

When morning comes here on the third day, it's raining. Walter Husband emerges from his tent here at base camp and is rushing around gathering up his clothes and writing material left outside on the folding tables they brought with them. He manages to bring all of it into the tent before the rainwater can get them wet. The crew of photographers is putting up the giant umbrellas and using special made covers to put over the camera equipment so they can still take pictures. Coshocton has already started the new lead. In addition, he is at a place up the mountainside that has some flakes. He is driving spikes into them and the flakes spread more wide when he does. It has the pitons loosely where he placed them and attached his rope.

"Coshocton, are you sure about those safes? Because the pitons are too wobbly like that," says Donna, still coming up from behind him.

"I've been this way before, they'll hold out. Besides, we only have four more pitches to go. Tomorrow's our fourth day and that'll be it."

They are all at a place where they can only hang by their ropes. Because there's no ledges and there's very few handholds and footholds nor is there a stance where they can place their feet to get better support from their legs. The force of the rain coming down on them with high winds is weight. Moreover, it makes it hard for them to see. There are places in the mountainside that has the rainwater like little waterfalls and little fast moving creeks and streams.

"This rain may keep up all day," Ben shouts.

"Everybody keeps moving," Coshocton commanded.

The photographers below and Walter

Husband are all in their raingear busying themselves with picture taking.

"The rain coming down on them is more than I had hopped for," Walter husband replies.

"Oh yes, these will be outstanding pictures of real mountain climbers upon a mountain in the rain," says one of the photographers.

"It all adds new life to what I'm doing," says Walter.

Several hours pass and the rain stops. Roy, like Coshocton, is using his hand-drill and hammer to make a hole to place the pitons. He is leading Milton across a blank traverse to meet up with the rest of them. It's been two pitches now, and they've all decided to set up their hammocks and hang there, sleeping the night through. The final pictures are taken of the mountain climbers as they hang there in suspended animation.

The night air is cool, especially since after the rain. During the day here in the summer-time El Capitan gets very hot in the sun, almost too hot to bear. Coshocton and his team know to climb the mountain in the fall. However, what brings them here now is

the payment they will receive from Walter Husband. In the dark, you can see into the Twilight from high up on a mountain. And in the Twilight you can see zones of stars like images that one can imagine beyond one's wildest dreams. Everyone is asleep hanging in a hammock now, and some are sleeping in a tent at base camp.

On the third day of climbing El Capitan, all of a sudden here in the middle of the night, a hammock rips out of the wall, and drops down to a ledge from the second day. And the thump from the hard hitting fall knocks the wind out of the sleeper and severely hurts his back. A deep grunting and long blast of air, as though pressure is released from a valve, comes from the fallen one. He lies there all night long in excruciating pain—unable to cry out for help. It's out of the twilight now, and into the new sun. Donna awakens and rises half up in her hammock. Sitting up with her legs stretched out in front of her, she stretches her arms up into the air, yawning. She gets herself all back and looks out into the open air, then looks down. A loud scream comes from

deep within Donna and fills the endless skies. The rest of them come to life with excitement, and are quick to look in the direction of the screaming.

"What is it?! What happened?!" Roy cries out.

"Look down there on the ledge! Do you see him?! It's Coshocton! His pitons must have ripped out!" she answers.

"I'll call base camp, all of us shouldn't get on the cell phone all at once, just let me do it," says Milton.

He is able to collect himself better than the others.

"He's reaching up to us!" shouts Donna.

"I'm going down there," Ben chimes in.

The pitch is cleaned up enough that Ben can use ropes already established to go down to where Coshocton is and help him.

"Hey Coshocton, it's me, Ben."

"I can see it's you. I'm without a rope. Put a piton there in the crack and fix me up a safe line."

"Ok, Milton called base and the rescue helicopter should be here anytime, so why don't you just keep still until it gets here?"

"That's ok, I'll still make the climb and I know it."

"Are you kidding me man? You must have fallen without knowing it and that's got to be pretty bad."

"Just give me the rope now and I'm climbing up. It won't take long to get to where we were, since there's a line already there. You see, I'm standing now, and look, there goes my hammock in the wind."

"Coshocton, what are you going to do, are you climbing back up?" Donna shouts down at him.

"Yes, he feels he can still finish it!" Ben shouts up to her.

"You go ahead first Ben," says Coshocton.

"Ok, but you look bad, man."

Coshocton reaches up with his hands and steps up with one leg.

"Oooosh!"

He sounds a loud painful sound. His back is hurting him very badly.

"Are you sure man?!" asks Ben looking back at him excited.

"Yes I'm sure, its pain in my back from the fall. It'll get good enough once I get ta moving around a bit."

"Coshocton, maybe you should wait for the copter!" Milton calls down to him.

"I can still make it, just you hang on!"

He gets to the top of the first pitch when the helicopter arrives. It's hovering at the face of the mountain in front of them, keeping enough distance away so as not to get to close with the propelling blades. The crew can see Coshocton is the one hurt. Because he is in a lot of pain climbing up the face of the mountain using the rope. Finally, Coshocton and Ben join the rest of the team at the top of the second pitch.

"Coshocton, are you sure, you want me to send the rescue copter away?" asks Milton.

"Yes, I'm sure."

They're over hanging and will assist Coshocton with the rest of the climb. The rescue helicopter goes back to its holding place. They make it to the top by nightfall, and throw their haul bags off the top of El Capitan. That is the custom for climbers when they finish the climb. The helicopter comes back for Coshocton.

"I told you, I'll be there at the top of the

mountain," he says after they lay him down on the stretcher.

His team walks down to the valley using one of those trails there. And Walter Husband is filled up with more unexpected pictures than he had ever dreamed.

Epilogue

In Moab Utah, Allen Memorial Hospital is advanced with its scientific research. Within its domains Arnold Caldwell is lying in his hospital bed and has his mother and father to watch over him along with Joyce. "Good morning doctor," replies Joyce standing there at Arnolds head as the doctor steps in. "Good morning," says the doctor. "Arnold and Mr. and Mrs. Caldwell, this is doctor Chow Lin from China. He'll be performing the operation on Arnold's clubfoot."

In a room just beneath Arnold, down on the next floor, lies Coshocton Dulge. He too is in his hospital bed and has Irene by his side. Because of his being an urgent matter, the examiners came very quickly for him. After the helicopter brought Coshocton down the mountain and into the valley, he was immediately flown home from Yosemite Valley. The doctor explains to him and Irene that Coshocton will be in a body cast for a while after surgery. He'll have to get pins installed in his back, because his vertebrate is so badly damaged. And when the cast comes off he'll need to have the steel crutches to help stand and walk on his legs. It is as though Coshocton Dulge and Arnold Caldwell traded places.

Still, Irene and Coshocton will marry.

www.ingramcontent.com/pod-product-compliance
Ingram Content Group UK Ltd.
Pitfield, Milton Keynes, MK11 3LW, UK
UKHW040019200726
13854UKWH00001B/272

9 781425 155391